Let's Get Powered Up

The Masti Brother Adventures

Zarina Rasheed

Let's Get Powered Up
Copyright © 2024 by Zarina Rasheed

All rights reserved. No part of this publication may be reproduced, distributed, or transmitted in any form or by any means, including photocopying, recording, or other electronic or mechanical methods, without the prior written permission of the author, except in the case of brief quotations embodied in critical reviews and certain other non-commercial uses permitted by copyright law.

Tellwell Talent
www.tellwell.ca

ISBN
978-0-2288-9668-5 (Paperback)
978-0-2288-9669-2 (eBook)

To my constant inspiration, Imran.
You show me every day that your
spirit is forever unbreakable.

Aamir and Imran are always looking for something fun to do. Since they live next door to each other it's easy for them to plan their adventures whenever they want.

Aamir loves basketball and tennis. He knows one day he will go pro like James Hardin.

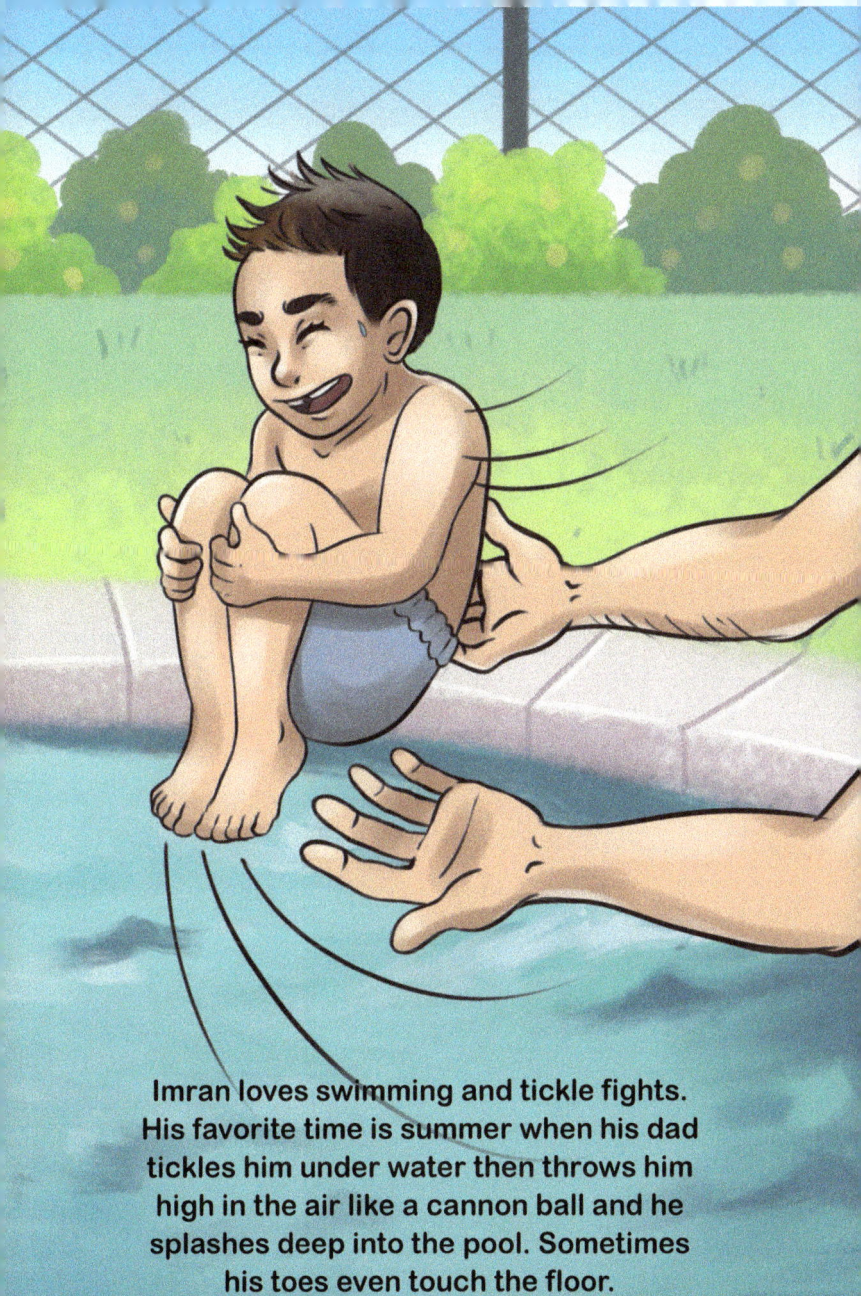

Imran loves swimming and tickle fights. His favorite time is summer when his dad tickles him under water then throws him high in the air like a cannon ball and he splashes deep into the pool. Sometimes his toes even touch the floor.

From playing hide and seek, to chasing imaginary dragons out of the house, and even building huge forts in the living room, these two love a good adventure.

They even have secret special powers.
Imran can run at lightning speed
and Aamir can turn invisible.

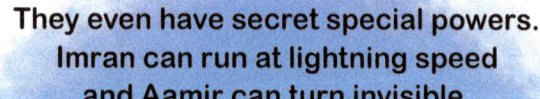

Even Max, their super dog, can fly!

They came over the day before to make sure he has all his superpower items for the big day:

a. Supersonic speed tablet for all the number one movies: check
b. Super soft blanket to keep him warm: check
c. Super awesome snacks in case of energy shortage: check
d. Super high-speed watch to keep track of infusion time: check

Looks like they are all set for the big day tomorrow.

Imran's mom and dad make sure to plan a fun morning before they go, and they always pick up a surprise for the superhero helpers at the hospital. Today they decide to go with VANILLA CUPCAKES WITH SPRINKLES—Imran's favorite. He's sure his mom will get an extra just for him.

After they unload all the super gear and get settled in their private headquarters, Imran and his mom pick what movies to watch first.

Even though it can feel like *FOREVER* to get his bone juice, it is worth the wait so all of Imran's superpowers can be restored. Sometimes, to make the time pass faster, he takes a snooze with his mom. Even superheroes need to sleep sometimes!

His mom tells him that this bone juice is necessary so his soft bones can get extra strong, and he can go on more adventures with Max and Aamir. He knows she is right because he always feels extra powerful the next day.

Aamir, Max, and Imran decide to start planning their next adventure now that Imran is all powered up! Until their next Masti Brother Adventure…

www.ingramcontent.com/pod-product-compliance
Lightning Source LLC
LaVergne TN
LVHW072023060526
838200LV00058B/4662